Legacy of Darkness

Andrew Lancaster and The Olympians, Volume 2

Tharun Vigneswar PS

Published by Tharun Vigneswar PS, 2024.

LEGACY OF DARKNESS

First edition. July 15, 2024.

Copyright © 2024 Tharun Vigneswar PS.

ISBN: 979-8227918598

Written by Tharun Vigneswar PS.

Table of Contents

Chapter 1

THE GATHERING STORM

Under the canopy of stars, Andrew Lancaster stood alongside his companions, a sense of purpose settling over him like a comforting cloak. The events of the past year had tested their mettle and forged bonds that would endure the trials yet to come. But as they stood together in the heart of Camp Half-Blood, Andrew couldn't shake the feeling that their greatest challenges still lay ahead.

The victory over their previous adversaries had brought temporary respite, but Andrew knew that peace was fleeting in the world of demigods. The shadows of the past loomed large, and whispers of Kronos' return haunted their every step.

As the campfires burned bright, casting flickering shadows across the faces of his friends, Andrew found himself lost in thought. The battles they had fought, the sacrifices they had made—they all seemed like distant memories now, overshadowed by the looming threat of the Titan lord.

But amidst the uncertainty, a glimmer of hope remained. For in the heart of Camp Half-Blood, surrounded by friends who had become like family, Andrew knew that he had found his home. A place where heroes were forged, destinies were realized, and the bonds of friendship were unbreakable.

As the night wore on, a sense of foreboding settled over the camp, mirroring the turmoil in Andrew's heart. The stars above seemed to shimmer with an otherworldly light, casting an eerie glow over the gathering.

And then, as if in response to their silent fears, a messenger arrived bearing news that would change everything. The prophecies had spoken, and the signs were clear: Kronos was rising, and the fate of Olympus hung in the balance.

With a heavy heart, Andrew turned to his companions, their faces etched with determination. The time for action had come, and they would face the challenges ahead with courage and resolve.

For as the first rumblings of the gathering storm echoed through the night, Andrew and his companions stood ready to confront the darkness that threatened to engulf them all. And though the road ahead would be fraught with danger and uncertainty, they knew that together, they would emerge stronger, united by their shared determination to protect all that they held dear.

As dawn broke over Camp Half-Blood, casting a golden glow over the sprawling grounds, Andrew Lancaster and his companions found themselves thrust into a new reality—one fraught with uncertainty and danger. The weight of the impending conflict hung heavy in the air, casting a somber shadow over the once vibrant camp.

Gathered in the central square, demigods from all corners of the camp listened intently as Andrew addressed them, his voice steady despite the gravity of the situation. He spoke of the challenges they would face, of the sacrifices that would be required, but also of the hope that burned bright within their hearts.

"We stand on the brink of war," Andrew declared, his words echoing off the stone walls of the surrounding buildings. "But we do not stand alone. Together, we will face whatever darkness comes our way, and emerge victorious against the greatest evil the world has ever known."

His companions stood beside him, their faces set with determination as they pledged their allegiance to the cause. Kiara, daughter of Poseidon, her eyes reflecting the endless depths of the ocean. Adrian, son of Hephaestus, his hands already itching to forge new weapons for the coming battle. Harry, son of Hades, his gaze steady despite the weight of his dark heritage. And Michael, the loyal satyr, his hooves planted firmly on the ground as he stood ready to defend his charges.

As the sun rose higher in the sky, casting long shadows across the camp, Andrew knew that their journey was only just beginning. The road ahead would be fraught with peril, but he was determined to lead his fellow demigods with courage and resolve.

For as the first rays of sunlight illuminated the camp, Andrew Lancaster and his companions stood ready to confront the gathering storm, united in their determination to protect all that they held dear. And though the path ahead would be fraught with danger and uncertainty, they knew that together, they would emerge stronger, their bonds forged in the crucible of battle, ready to face whatever challenges awaited them.

As the morning sun continued its ascent, bathing Camp Half-Blood in a warm glow, Andrew Lancaster and his companions wasted no time in springing into action. With a sense of urgency pulsing through the air, they dispersed throughout the camp, rallying their fellow demigods and preparing them for the trials that lay ahead.

Andrew's first task was to consult with Chiron, the wise centaur who had guided him through countless challenges. Together, they pored over ancient scrolls and prophecies, searching for any clues that might shed light on Kronos' plans and how they could best prepare to face him.

Meanwhile, Kiara, Adrian, Harry, and Michael fanned out across the camp, each taking on their own responsibilities in the preparations for war. Kiara organized combat drills by the lake, honing the demigods' skills in water-based combat. Adrian set up a makeshift forge, crafting weapons and armor to arm their forces for the coming battle. Harry ventured into the depths of the underworld, seeking guidance from his father and preparing to harness his powers in the fight against Kronos. And Michael, ever vigilant, patrolled the camp's borders, ensuring that they remained secure against any potential threats.

As the day wore on, the sense of urgency only grew stronger, fueled by the knowledge that Kronos' forces could strike at any moment. But amidst the chaos and uncertainty, a sense of camaraderie and determination prevailed. Demigods from all corners of the camp came together, united in their resolve to defend their home and the world beyond.

As evening fell and the campfires flickered to life, Andrew gathered his companions once more, their faces illuminated by the warm glow of the flames. With a sense of grim determination, they shared a silent vow—to stand together against the darkness, no matter the cost.

As the night deepened and the camp settled into an uneasy stillness, Andrew found himself alone with his thoughts, gazing up at the stars that punctuated the dark canvas of the sky. The weight of responsibility bore down on him like a heavy cloak, reminding him of the daunting task that lay ahead.

Despite the flickering flames of the campfires and the reassuring presence of his companions nearby, Andrew couldn't shake the feeling of uncertainty that gnawed at his insides. The prophecy of Kronos' return echoed in his mind, a constant reminder of the imminent danger they faced.

But even in the face of such overwhelming odds, Andrew refused to succumb to despair. He drew strength from the memories of past victories, from the bonds of friendship that had sustained them through countless trials. And above all, he clung to the belief that together, they could overcome any obstacle, no matter how insurmountable it seemed.

As he stood alone in the quiet of the night, Andrew made a silent vow to himself and to his companions. He swore to lead them with courage and conviction, to stand firm in the face of adversity, and to never waver in their quest to protect all that they held dear.

With renewed determination burning in his heart, Andrew turned his gaze back to the camp below, where the flickering lights of the campfires illuminated the faces of his fellow demigods. The time for action had come, and he was ready to face whatever challenges awaited them, united in their shared purpose and bound by the unbreakable bonds of friendship.

For as the night wore on and the stars continued their silent vigil, Andrew Lancaster knew that the gathering storm would test them in ways they had never imagined. But with hope as their beacon and courage as their guide, they would stand tall against the darkness, ready to confront their destiny and forge a future where light triumphed over shadow, and where hope endured in the face of despair.

Chapter 2

THE RISE OF KRONOS

In the heart of the underworld, where shadows danced and whispers of ancient power echoed through the void, a malevolent force stirred. Deep within the depths of Tartarus, where the darkness held sway and the chains of fate lay coiled, Kronos, the Titan lord, began to awaken from his slumber.

As he emerged from the depths of Tartarus, his presence sent tremors through the fabric of reality itself. The very air crackled with dark energy as he took his first steps into the world of mortals, his form wreathed in shadow and his eyes burning with an unholy fire.

With a triumphant roar that echoed through the underworld, Kronos called forth his loyal followers—Titans who had slumbered in the depths of Tartarus for millennia, awaiting the day when their master would rise again. Together, they rallied to his side, their ranks swelling with each passing moment as they prepared to unleash their fury upon the world above.

As rumors of Kronos' return spread like wildfire across the mortal realm, fear and uncertainty gripped the hearts of men and gods alike. Whispers of his plans to overthrow Olympus and seize control of the heavens sent shockwaves through the divine realm, prompting gods and demigods alike to brace themselves for the coming storm.

In Camp Half-Blood, the news of Kronos' resurgence sent a shiver down Andrew Lancaster's spine. The prophecy had spoken of the Titan lord's return, but even he had not dared to imagine the full extent of the threat they now faced. With each passing moment, the sense of urgency grew more palpable, driving Andrew and his companions to redouble their efforts in preparation for the inevitable clash.

As the sun dipped below the horizon and darkness descended upon the camp, Andrew gathered his companions once more, their faces grave as they discussed their next course of action. They knew that the time for hesitation had passed—the rise of Kronos heralded a new era of darkness, one that threatened to engulf them all if they did not act swiftly.

With grim determination etched upon their features, Andrew and his companions set out to rally their fellow demigods and prepare them for the battles that lay ahead. They knew that the road ahead would be fraught with peril, but they also knew that they could not afford to falter in the face of such a formidable foe.

As they worked tirelessly into the night, the echoes of Kronos' triumphant roar reverberated through the air, a chilling reminder of the perilous path that lay before them. But even as the darkness threatened to consume them, Andrew and his companions stood resolute, their hearts filled with courage and their spirits unbroken, ready to face whatever challenges awaited them in the coming days.

For as the stars twinkled overhead, casting their steady light upon the camp, Andrew Lancaster and his companions knew that the rise of Kronos marked the beginning of a battle that would shape the fate of the world itself. And though the road ahead would be fraught with danger and uncertainty, they stood ready to confront their destiny with unwavering resolve, united in their determination to protect all that they held dear.

In the dead of night, as Andrew's weary body succumbed to the embrace of sleep, his mind drifted into the realm of dreams.

But instead of finding solace in the comforting embrace of slumber, he found himself plunged into a world of darkness, where shadows danced and whispers of ancient power echoed through the void.

It was there, amidst the shifting sands of his dreams, that Kronos appeared before him—a towering figure wreathed in shadow, his eyes burning with a malevolent light. With a voice that reverberated through the depths of Andrew's soul, the Titan lord spoke, his words dripping with honeyed venom.

"Andrew Lancaster," Kronos intoned, his voice like the rumble of distant thunder. "I have watched you from the depths of Tartarus, and I know of your struggles. Join me, and together we can forge a new world—one where mortals and gods alike will kneel before our might."

Andrew's heart hammered in his chest as he stared into the abyssal depths of Kronos' eyes, feeling the weight of the Titan lord's words pressing down upon him like a suffocating blanket. The offer was tempting, he couldn't deny it—the promise of power, of glory, of a world remade in their image.

But deep down, Andrew knew that to accept Kronos' offer would mean betraying everything he held dear. His friends, his allies, his very sense of self—all would be sacrificed in service to a dark and twisted cause. And so, with a strength born of conviction, he found the courage to speak.

"No," Andrew declared, his voice ringing out clear and true in the darkness. "I will not betray my friends, nor will I forsake the principles that define who I am. Your offer may be tempting, Kronos, but I will not be swayed by promises of power. My loyalty lies with those who fight for the light, not those who seek to extinguish it."

As the echoes of his words faded into the void, Andrew watched as Kronos' form wavered and flickered like a flame in the wind, his eyes burning with rage. But even as the Titan lord vanished into the darkness, Andrew knew that the battle was far from over. The true test of his resolve lay ahead, and he would face it with unwavering determination, ready to confront whatever darkness awaited him in the waking world.

With a start, Andrew's eyes snapped open, his heart still racing from the intensity of his dream. As he blinked away the remnants of sleep, the memories of Kronos' sinister offer lingered like a dark cloud overhead. But even as the specter of doubt threatened to cloud his thoughts, Andrew drew strength from the knowledge that he had stood firm in the face of temptation.

Pushing himself upright, Andrew took a deep breath, willing the lingering tendrils of darkness to dissipate. He knew that dwelling on the events of his dream would only serve to distract him from the task at hand. There was much to be done, and he could ill afford to lose himself in uncertainty.

Rising from his cot, Andrew made his way through the dimly lit cabin, his mind already racing with plans and strategies. Outside, the first light of dawn painted the sky in hues of pink and gold, casting a warm glow over the campgrounds. The sounds of morning activity filled the air, a comforting symphony that served as a reminder of the life that thrived within the walls of Camp Half-Blood.

Descending the steps of the cabin, Andrew found himself drawn towards the familiar sight of the pavilion, where breakfast was already being served. The scent of freshly cooked food wafted through the air, mingling with the chatter of demigods as they gathered to break their fast.

Taking his place at the table, Andrew greeted his friends with a nod, their eyes meeting in silent understanding. Though the events of the night still weighed heavily on his mind, he knew that he could count on their unwavering support. Together, they would face whatever challenges lay ahead, united in their determination to stand against the darkness.

As he reached for a plate of food, Andrew felt a sense of calm settle over him. The road ahead would be long and treacherous, but he knew that as long as they stood together, they would emerge victorious. With each bite of food, he fortified himself for the trials yet to come, ready to confront whatever darkness awaited them with courage and resolve.

After finishing his meal, Andrew sought out Chiron, the wise centaur who served as mentor and guide to the demigods of Camp Half-Blood. Finding him in his usual spot near the edge of the training grounds, Andrew approached, his mind still troubled by the events of his dream.

"Chiron," Andrew began, his voice betraying the lingering unease he felt. "I had a dream last night—a vision, perhaps. Kronos appeared to me, offering me and my friends a place in his army. He tried to convince me to join him, but I refused."

Chiron regarded Andrew with a thoughtful expression, his gaze piercing as he listened to the young demigod's words. After a moment of silence, he spoke, his voice calm and reassuring.

"Andrew, what you experienced is not uncommon among demigods," Chiron explained, his tone gentle but firm. "Dreams have long been a conduit for divine messages and visions, and it is not unusual for beings such as Kronos to attempt to sway mortals to their cause through such means."

Andrew nodded, absorbing Chiron's words with a sense of relief. Though he had suspected as much, hearing it confirmed by the centaur's wisdom helped to ease the lingering doubts that had plagued him since waking.

"Does this mean that Kronos is truly rising, then?" Andrew asked, his voice tinged with concern.

Chiron nodded gravely. "It would seem so. The signs are unmistakable, and we must prepare ourselves for the inevitable conflict that lies ahead. But take heart, Andrew. You have shown great strength and resolve in resisting Kronos' temptations, and that is a testament to your character."

With a grateful nod, Andrew thanked Chiron for his guidance, feeling a renewed sense of determination settle over him. Though the road ahead would be fraught with danger, he knew that he was not alone. With the support of his friends and the wisdom of his mentor, he would face whatever challenges awaited him with courage and conviction.

Leaving Chiron's side, Andrew felt a weight lift from his shoulders. The centaur's reassurance had brought him a sense of clarity and purpose, reaffirming his resolve to stand against the rising threat of Kronos.

As he made his way through the camp, Andrew's thoughts turned to his friends—Kiara, Adrian, Harry, and Michael. They had been with him through thick and thin, their unwavering loyalty serving as a constant source of strength. He knew that together, they would face whatever challenges lay ahead, united in their determination to protect the world they called home.

Reaching the edge of the training grounds, Andrew spotted his companions gathered together, their faces alight with determination. Without hesitation, he joined them, his heart swelling with pride at the sight of their camaraderie.

"Friends," Andrew began, his voice steady and resolute. "Last night, I had a vision—a warning, perhaps, of the dangers that lie ahead. Kronos is rising, and with him comes the threat of war. But we will not cower in fear. We will stand together, as we always have, and face this challenge head-on."

His friends nodded in agreement, their expressions mirroring Andrew's determination. They knew that the road ahead would be fraught with peril, but they also knew that they would face it together, bound by the unbreakable bonds of friendship and loyalty.

With their resolve renewed, Andrew and his companions set to work, preparing themselves for the battles that lay ahead. They trained tirelessly, honing their skills and strategizing for the coming conflict. And as the sun dipped below the horizon, casting long shadows across the campgrounds, they stood united, ready to confront whatever darkness awaited them with courage and conviction.

For as long as they stood together, Andrew knew that they would emerge victorious, their spirits unbroken and their hearts filled with hope. And with each passing moment, the bond between them grew stronger, a beacon of light in the gathering storm.

Chapter 3

A CALL TO ARMS

In the resplendent halls of Olympus, where the very air thrummed with divine energy, Andrew and his companions stood amidst the council of gods, their expressions grave as they prepared to address the looming threat of Kronos and his Titans. The grandeur of their surroundings served as a stark reminder of the weight of their task— to rally allies and prepare for war against an ancient and formidable enemy.

Zeus, his countenance stern and commanding, presided over the assembly, his voice resonating with authority as he addressed the gathered immortals. "We stand at the precipice of a great conflict," he declared, his words carrying the weight of centuries of rule. "Kronos has risen, and with him, the threat of unimaginable destruction. We must act swiftly and decisively if we are to stand any chance of victory."

The gods listened intently as Andrew and his companions outlined the urgency of the situation, their voices echoing with the determination of those who knew the gravity of the task before them. As they spoke of the need to gather allies and prepare for war, the magnitude of the threat became increasingly clear, tensions rising among the assembled immortals.

"We cannot face this threat alone," Athena, goddess of wisdom, interjected, her voice measured but resolute. "We must seek out allies who share our cause, who understand the stakes of this conflict and are willing to stand with us against the forces of darkness."

Her words were met with murmurs of agreement from the council, each member recognizing the importance of solidarity in the face of such a formidable adversary. But even as they discussed potential allies, tensions simmered beneath the surface, old rivalries and grievances threatening to fracture their unity.

"We must also be wary of potential threats," Apollo, god of prophecy, cautioned, his expression grave. "Kronos may have allies of his own, and we cannot afford to underestimate the reach of his influence."

His words cast a shadow over the assembly, a reminder of the dangers that lurked beyond the safety of Olympus' walls. Yet, even in the face of uncertainty, Andrew and his companions remained resolute, their determination unwavering as they pledged to do whatever it took to ensure the safety of their world.

As the discussion continued, plans were made to reach out to potential allies, to seek out those who would stand beside them in the coming conflict. From the demigods of Camp Half-Blood to the ancient warriors of distant lands, they sought out those who shared their vision of a world free from tyranny and oppression.

But even as they worked to forge alliances, tensions ran high among the assembled immortals, each member keenly aware of the stakes of the conflict that lay ahead.

As the council of gods and demigods deliberated on their strategy, names of potential allies were whispered in hushed tones, each one carrying with it the weight of destiny.

Ares, the god of war, stood tall and imposing, his gaze piercing as he spoke of rallying the fiercest warriors from the farthest corners of the mortal realm. "We shall seek out the mightiest champions," he declared, his voice resonating with the thunderous clamor of battle.

"Those whose names strike fear into the hearts of their enemies, whose valor knows no bounds."

Beside him, Artemis, the goddess of the hunt, nodded in agreement, her expression steely as she spoke of enlisting the aid of her loyal hunters. "The daughters of Artemis shall join the fray," she proclaimed, her voice ringing clear and true. "With bow in hand and heart aflame, they shall stand as guardians of the natural world, defenders of all that is pure and untamed."

But it was not just the gods of war and the hunt who pledged their support. From the depths of the sea, Poseidon, god of the oceans, offered the aid of his loyal subjects—the Nereids and Tritons who dwelled beneath the waves. "The seas shall rise in our defense," he vowed, his voice carrying the weight of the crashing waves. "With trident in hand and tempest at their command, they shall sweep away our enemies like chaff before the storm."

And so, as the names of warriors and minor gods were spoken, a sense of purpose settled over the assembly, a shared understanding of the task that lay ahead. For they knew that in the face of such a formidable foe, they would need all the allies they could muster if they were to emerge victorious.

But even as plans were made and alliances forged, tensions lingered in the air, a reminder of the challenges that lay ahead. For the road to victory would be long and fraught with peril, and the fate of Olympus and all of existence hung in the balance.

As the discussion unfolded, more names were added to the roster of potential allies, each one representing a glimmer of hope in the encroaching darkness.

Hermes, the messenger of the gods, spoke of enlisting the aid of his swift-footed children—those demigods blessed with speed and agility, capable of delivering messages and outmaneuvering their foes on the battlefield. "With their unmatched swiftness, they shall serve as our eyes and ears," he declared, his voice quick and lively. "No secret shall elude their grasp, no enemy shall escape their pursuit."

Beside him, Hestia, goddess of the hearth, offered the support of her peaceful domain—the humble hearths and warm hearts of mortals who welcomed weary travelers and offered solace to the downtrodden. "In times of strife, it is the bonds of family and community that sustain us," she proclaimed, her voice gentle and reassuring. "We shall seek out those who offer kindness and hospitality, for in their embrace, we shall find strength and comfort."

And from the shadows, Hecate, goddess of magic and crossroads, whispered of enlisting the aid of her followers—the witches and sorcerers who wielded the powers of the arcane and walked the paths between worlds. "In the darkness of night, our allies shall weave their spells," she murmured, her voice like a haunting melody. "Their magic shall be our shield, their knowledge our guide."

As each god and goddess pledged their support and offered the aid of their loyal subjects, a sense of unity began to take root among the assembled immortals. For though they hailed from different domains and held divergent beliefs, they were united by a common purpose—the defense of Olympus and the preservation of all they held dear.

But even as plans were made and alliances forged, tensions lingered in the air, a reminder of the challenges that lay ahead. For the road to victory would be long and fraught with peril, and the fate of Olympus and all of existence hung in the balance.

But even as plans were made and alliances forged, tensions simmered beneath the surface, a reflection of the uncertainty that hung over the council like a shadow. For though they spoke of unity and solidarity, the gods and demigods knew that old grudges and rivalries could easily resurface in times of crisis.

"It is not enough to simply gather allies," Athena, the goddess of wisdom, interjected, her voice cutting through the murmurs of the assembly. "We must also devise a strategy—a plan of action that will enable us to face our enemies with strength and determination."

Her words struck a chord with the assembled immortals, a reminder of the importance of foresight and planning in the face of such a formidable foe. And so, as the council continued their deliberations, they began to map out the steps that would lead them to victory.

From the shores of distant lands to the depths of the underworld, the gods and demigods reached out to potential allies, their messages carried on the wings of Hermes' fleet-footed messengers. Each emissary returned with tales of hope and promise, of warriors and minor gods who stood ready to join the fight against Kronos and his Titans.

As the discussions progressed, the focus shifted to devising a comprehensive plan to defend Olympus against the impending threat of Kronos and his forces. The gods and demigods gathered around a vast map of the celestial realm, their brows furrowed in concentration as they debated the best course of action.

"We must fortify the borders of Olympus," Athena declared, her voice steady and commanding. "We cannot allow our enemies to breach our defenses unchallenged. We must bolster our armies, reinforce our fortifications, and stand ready to repel any assault with strength and resolve."

Her words were met with murmurs of agreement from the assembled immortals, each one recognizing the importance of securing their home against the looming threat. Plans were quickly set in motion to station guards at key checkpoints, to strengthen the magical barriers that protected Olympus from intrusion, and to prepare for the possibility of a siege.

But defense alone would not be enough to ensure their victory. Hermes, ever the strategist, proposed a more proactive approach. "We must take the fight to Kronos," he suggested, his eyes gleaming with determination. "We cannot afford to wait for him to strike first. We must gather our forces, launch preemptive strikes against his strongholds, and disrupt his plans before they can come to fruition."

His proposal sparked a lively debate among the council, with some arguing for caution and others advocating for bold action. But in the end, it was decided that a combination of defense and offense would be the most effective strategy—a two-pronged approach that would keep their enemies off-balance and give them the best chance of victory.

Athena, with her strategic acumen, meticulously divided the assembled army, ensuring that each god and goddess played a vital role in the defense of Olympus. As the councilors took their places, she began to outline the responsibilities of each unit, taking into account their unique strengths and abilities.

The first unit, led by the war god Ares and the huntress Artemis, would form the vanguard of their defense. Ares, with his ferocity and martial prowess, would lead the charge into battle, his mighty sword cleaving through the ranks of their enemies. At his side, Artemis and her loyal Hunters would provide invaluable support, their precision archery and unparalleled tracking skills turning the tide of battle in their favor.

The second unit, entrusted to the care of Hermes and Hestia, would be responsible for protecting the civilians and non-combatants of Olympus. Hermes, with his unmatched speed and agility, would coordinate the evacuation efforts, ensuring that the vulnerable members of their community were safely escorted to designated shelters. Meanwhile, Hestia, with her gentle demeanor and nurturing spirit, would provide comfort and solace to those in need, her warm hearths serving as beacons of hope in the darkness.

The third unit, under the guidance of Dionysus and Hecate, would specialize in guerrilla warfare and sabotage. Dionysus, with his ability to inspire madness and revelry, would lead daring raids against the enemy's supply lines and outposts, spreading chaos and confusion among their ranks. Hecate, mistress of magic and mistress of the crossroads, would weave her spells to conceal their movements and confound their enemies, ensuring that they struck swiftly and silently, like shadows in the night.

And finally, the fourth unit, led by Athena herself, would serve as the linchpin of their defense, coordinating the efforts of the other units and formulating strategies to outwit their foes. With her keen intellect and strategic insight, Athena would lead their forces into battle, her unwavering determination inspiring courage and resolve in all who followed her.

With a resounding clap of thunder, Zeus, the king of the gods, rose from his throne and addressed Andrew and his companions with solemn gravity.

"Andrew Lancaster, son of Athena, and esteemed allies," Zeus intoned, his voice booming throughout the grand hall of Olympus. "I entrust upon you a sacred quest—a mission of utmost importance to the defense of Olympus and the preservation of our way of life."

Andrew and his friends listened intently, their hearts swelling with a sense of duty and purpose as the weight of Zeus's words settled upon them.

"You are to venture forth into the mortal world," Zeus continued, his gaze piercing and unwavering. "Seek out potential allies who may aid us in our time of need. Rally the forces of good to our cause, and together, we shall stand against the darkness that threatens to engulf us."

The gravity of their task hung heavy in the air as Andrew and his companions exchanged determined glances, their resolve steeled by the magnitude of the quest before them.

"Andrew Lancaster," Zeus said, fixing his gaze upon the young demigod. "You shall lead this quest, for your courage and leadership have proven to be unmatched among your peers. May the wisdom of Athena guide your steps, and may the strength of Olympus be with you."

With a solemn nod of acknowledgment, Andrew accepted the mantle of leadership, his heart swelling with pride and determination.

"Go forth, my children," Zeus declared, his voice echoing through the halls of Olympus. "And may your quest be met with success. The fate of Olympus rests in your hands."

And so, with Zeus's blessing and the weight of their mission heavy upon their shoulders, Andrew and his companions set out from the lofty heights of Olympus, their hearts filled with determination and their minds set on the task ahead. For they knew that the fate of Olympus—and indeed, the fate of all existence—hung in the balance, and it was up to them to ensure that the forces of good prevailed against the encroaching darkness.

Chapter 4

ALLIES AND ENEMIES

As Andrew and his companions embarked on their quest to seek out potential allies, they traversed through the mortal world, their hearts filled with determination and their minds focused on the task at hand. Guided by the wisdom of Athena and the bonds of their friendship, they journeyed forth, their footsteps echoing with purpose and resolve.

Their first stop led them to the ancient city of Athens, where they sought an audience with the city's rulers and scholars. Andrew, with his lineage as a son of Athena, hoped to garner support from the mortal realm's most esteemed thinkers and strategists. However, they encountered unexpected resistance from those who harbored doubts about the existence of gods and demigods, their skepticism fueled by centuries of skepticism and disbelief.

Undeterred, Andrew and his companions pressed on, determined to prove their worth and win over the hearts and minds of the mortal populace. They embarked on a series of daring quests and heroic deeds, earning the respect and admiration of the people they encountered along the way. Yet, even as they gained allies among mortals, they encountered betrayal from unexpected quarters—agents of Kronos who sought to thwart their efforts and sow discord among their ranks.

It soon became clear that the influence of Kronos extended far beyond the realm of Olympus, reaching into the very fabric of mortal society. Dark forces conspired against them at every turn, threatening to undermine their quest and thwart their plans for victory.

But Andrew and his companions refused to yield to despair. United in purpose and bound by their unwavering determination, they stood firm against the tide of darkness, ready to face whatever challenges came their way.

As they continued their journey, the true extent of Kronos' influence began to reveal itself, casting a shadow of doubt and uncertainty over their path. Yet, with each obstacle they overcame and each ally they gained, they grew stronger in their resolve, their determination unshakeable in the face of adversity.

As Andrew and his companions journeyed through the mortal world in search of allies, they encountered a formidable challenge in the form of demi-titans—monstrous creatures with the blood of both gods and Titans coursing through their veins. These ancient beings, born of forbidden unions between gods and Titans, wielded powers that rivaled those of their divine ancestors.

The encounter with the demi-titans tested the limits of Andrew and his companions' strength and resolve. The battle was fierce and relentless, as the demi-titans unleashed their formidable powers upon them, their massive forms casting dark shadows over the battlefield.

But Andrew and his friends refused to back down in the face of adversity. With skillful tactics and unwavering determination, they fought bravely against their monstrous foes, their weapons flashing in the sunlight as they clashed with titanic strength and ferocity.

Kiara, daughter of Poseidon, summoned powerful waves to crash upon the shores of their enemies, using the very elements themselves to turn the tide of battle. Adrian, son of Hephaestus, crafted ingenious traps and weapons to ensnare and incapacitate their foes, his mechanical ingenuity proving to be a crucial asset in their struggle.

Harry, son of Hades, called upon the shadows themselves to cloak their movements and confound their enemies, his mastery over the darkness proving to be a potent weapon against the demi-titans. And Michael Chip, the stalwart satyr, fought valiantly at their side, using his agility and cunning to outmaneuver their enemies and strike at their weakest points.

Together, Andrew and his companions unleashed a relentless barrage of attacks upon the demi-titans, their combined efforts proving to be more than a match for their formidable foes. With each blow they struck, they drew closer to victory, their determination unyielding in the face of overwhelming odds.

And in the end, it was their unwavering courage and unity that carried them to triumph. As the last of the demi-titans fell beneath their combined onslaught, Andrew and his companions stood victorious, their spirits undaunted and their resolve unbroken.

For they knew that their journey was far from over, and that greater challenges lay ahead. But with each victory they achieved, they grew stronger in their conviction that together, they would overcome whatever obstacles stood in their way, and emerge victorious against the forces of darkness that threatened to engulf them all.

As Andrew and his companions pressed forward on their quest, they found themselves beset by a relentless onslaught of Kronos' minions. These dark creatures, twisted and corrupted by the malevolent influence of the Titan lord, sought to hinder their progress at every turn, their numbers seemingly endless as they swarmed forth from the shadows.

The minions of Kronos were varied and formidable, each one a testament to the depths of darkness that lurked within the heart of their master. From fearsome monsters to treacherous demigods, they threw themselves at Andrew and his companions with reckless abandon, their eyes burning with hatred and malice.

Yet, despite the overwhelming odds stacked against them, Andrew and his friends refused to yield to despair. With courage in their hearts and weapons in hand, they stood their ground against the tide of darkness, their resolve unshakeable in the face of adversity.

Kiara, daughter of Poseidon, summoned torrents of water to engulf their foes, her mastery over the seas proving to be a potent weapon against the minions of Kronos. Adrian, son of Hephaestus, forged barriers of fire and steel to hold back their advance, his engineering skills proving invaluable in their struggle.

Harry, son of Hades, wielded shadows like weapons, striking from the darkness with deadly precision to cut down their enemies where they stood. And Michael Chip, the steadfast satyr, danced through the fray with grace and agility, his hooves trampling their foes beneath him as he fought to protect his companions.

Together, Andrew and his friends fought with a ferocity born of desperation, each blow they struck driving back the forces of darkness inch by hard-won inch. Though they faced many trials and tribulations along the way, they refused to falter in their quest, knowing that the fate of Olympus—and indeed, the fate of all existence—hung in the balance.

And as they stood together on the battlefield, bathed in the glow of their hard-won victory, Andrew and his companions knew that their journey was far from over. For though they had faced many challenges and overcome many obstacles, they knew that the greatest trial still lay ahead—a final confrontation with the dark lord Kronos himself.

As the battle raged on, Andrew and his companions fought with unmatched determination, each clash with Kronos' minions bringing them closer to their ultimate goal. Yet, with every victory, they also grew more keenly aware of the enormity of the task that lay ahead.

Their path was fraught with danger at every turn, as they faced creatures of nightmare and demigods corrupted by the dark influence of Kronos. Each encounter tested their strength, their courage, and their unity as they fought against overwhelming odds.

But through it all, Andrew and his companions remained steadfast in their resolve, drawing strength from their bond and their shared purpose. With every blow they struck and every foe they vanquished, they moved one step closer to their destiny—to confront Kronos and put an end to his reign of terror once and for all.

And as they pressed forward, they could feel the weight of Olympus' hopes and dreams resting upon their shoulders. For they were not just fighting for themselves, but for the safety and security of all who called the realm of the gods their home.

With each victory, they gained valuable allies and resources, forging alliances with powerful beings who shared their desire to see Kronos defeated. Yet, they also encountered betrayal and treachery from unexpected quarters, as some sought to exploit the chaos for their own gain.

But through it all, Andrew and his companions remained resolute, their determination unwavering in the face of adversity. For they knew that the fate of Olympus—and indeed, the fate of all existence—hung in the balance, and that they alone held the power to tip the scales in favor of the light.

And so, with hearts filled with courage and minds set on their goal, they pressed onward, ready to face whatever challenges awaited them on their journey. For they knew that the road ahead would be long and perilous, but they also knew that they would face it together, as allies and friends united in their quest for victory.

As the battle raged on, Andrew and his companions fought with unmatched determination, each clash with Kronos' minions bringing them closer to their ultimate goal. Yet, with every victory, they also grew more keenly aware of the enormity of the task that lay ahead.

Their path was fraught with danger at every turn, as they faced creatures of nightmare and demigods corrupted by the dark influence of Kronos. Each encounter tested their strength, their courage, and their unity as they fought against overwhelming odds.

But through it all, Andrew and his companions remained steadfast in their resolve, drawing strength from their bond and their shared purpose. With every blow they struck and every foe they vanquished, they moved one step closer to their destiny—to confront Kronos and put an end to his reign of terror once and for all.

And as they pressed forward, they could feel the weight of Olympus' hopes and dreams resting upon their shoulders. For they were not just fighting for themselves, but for the safety and security of all who called the realm of the gods their home.

With each victory, they gained valuable allies and resources, forging alliances with powerful beings who shared their desire to see Kronos defeated. Yet, they also encountered betrayal and treachery from unexpected quarters, as some sought to exploit the chaos for their own gain.

But through it all, Andrew and his companions remained resolute, their determination unwavering in the face of adversity. For they knew that the fate of Olympus—and indeed, the fate of all existence—hung in the balance, and that they alone held the power to tip the scales in favor of the light.

And so, with hearts filled with courage and minds set on their goal, they pressed onward, ready to face whatever challenges awaited them on their journey. For they knew that the road ahead would be long and perilous, but they also knew that they would face it together, as allies and friends united in their quest for victory.

As Andrew and his companions ventured into Modern Athens, the ancient city's bustling streets greeted them with a cacophony of sights and sounds, a vibrant tapestry woven from the threads of history and modernity. Towering monuments and majestic statues bore silent witness to the city's storied past, while the hustle and bustle of everyday life echoed through its winding alleys and bustling markets.

Their first audience was with King Leonidas, a legendary figure whose name resonated with tales of heroism and valor. Clad in the armor of his forefathers, he stood before them with the quiet strength of a warrior who had faced countless battles and emerged victorious. With a firm handshake and a solemn nod, he pledged his unwavering support to Andrew and his companions, vowing to stand shoulder to shoulder with them in the coming war.

"Your cause is just, young heroes," King Leonidas declared, his voice carrying the weight of centuries of Spartan tradition. "We Spartans have long stood as guardians of freedom and justice, and we will not shirk from our duty now. My warriors will march with you into battle, and together, we will crush the forces of darkness that seek to enslave us all."

Next, they sought an audience with King Demetrius, a man of keen intellect and strategic brilliance whose name was whispered in hushed tones among the corridors of power. In the grand halls of his palace, adorned with tapestries depicting scenes of triumph and conquest, he listened intently to Andrew and his companions as they laid out their plans for the coming conflict.

"Ah, young heroes," King Demetrius said with a knowing smile, his eyes alight with the fire of ambition and determination. "You have come to the right place. Athens is a city of thinkers and warriors alike, and we shall lend our expertise to your cause. Together, we will devise a strategy that will outmaneuver even the most cunning of adversaries."

And finally, they were granted an audience with King Alexander, a charismatic and beloved ruler whose words had the power to move hearts and minds. In the opulent halls of his palace, adorned with golden trinkets and priceless treasures, he welcomed Andrew and his companions with open arms, his voice ringing out with the promise of hope and unity.

"My friends," King Alexander proclaimed, his voice carrying across the chamber like a clarion call. "In times of darkness, it is the light of unity and solidarity that shines brightest. Let us stand together as one, united in purpose and resolve, and we shall overcome whatever challenges lie ahead. For the fate of Olympus—and indeed, the fate of all mankind—rests in our hands."

And so, with the support of the kings of Athens firmly behind them, Andrew and his companions set out once more on their journey, their hearts filled with renewed hope and determination.

For they knew that with allies like these at their side, they stood ready to face whatever trials awaited them in the days to come.

Chapter 5

THE BATTLE BEGINS

As the kings of Athens pledged their alliances in the hallowed halls of the Olympian council, their words echoed with the weight of ancient oaths and noble intentions. Before the assembled gods and goddesses, they knelt in solemn reverence, their voices resounding with the clarity of purpose and the strength of conviction.

King Leonidas, his gaze unwavering as he spoke, vowed to dispatch his finest warriors to Camp Half-Blood, the training ground of heroes, where they would stand shoulder to shoulder with Andrew and his companions in defense of Olympus. With a salute to the heavens, he pledged the full might of Sparta to the cause of justice and freedom, his words ringing with the echoes of battles long past.

"My lord Zeus, noble Olympians," King Leonidas declared, his voice carrying across the chamber like a clarion call. "The warriors of Sparta stand ready to do battle against the forces of darkness that threaten our world. We shall send our finest demigods to Camp Half-Blood, where they will receive training and guidance in the arts of war. Together, we will forge a bond of steel and resolve that shall withstand even the mightiest of foes."

Next, King Demetrius stepped forward, his brow furrowed in thought as he considered the weight of his words. With a solemn nod to the gods and goddesses who watched over them, he spoke of strategy and tactics, of plans laid and alliances forged in the crucible of war.

"Great Olympians, lords and ladies of the pantheon," King Demetrius began, his voice measured and calm. "Athens shall not falter in the face of adversity. We shall dispatch our demigod soldiers to Camp Half-Blood, where they will train alongside their comrades in arms. But we shall also lend our expertise in matters of strategy and logistics, for victory in war is not won by strength alone, but by cunning and foresight."

And finally, King Alexander, his eyes ablaze with the fire of inspiration, stepped forward to offer his own pledge of allegiance to the cause. With a flourish of his hand and a smile upon his lips, he spoke of unity and solidarity, of the power of friendship and the bonds that bound them all together.

"Mighty Olympians, patrons of our world," King Alexander proclaimed, his voice carrying across the chamber like a symphony of hope and determination. "The people of Athens stand with you in this hour of need. We shall send our demigod soldiers to Camp Half-Blood, where they will stand as beacons of hope and courage in the face of darkness. Together, we shall forge a path to victory, guided by the light of justice and the strength of our convictions."

And so, with the pledges of the kings of Athens ringing in their ears, Andrew and his companions felt a renewed sense of purpose and determination. For they knew that with allies like these at their side, they stood ready to face whatever trials awaited them in the coming war against Kronos and his minions.

As the moon hung low in the night sky, casting an ethereal glow over Camp Half-Blood, Andrew found himself consumed by a restless sleep, his mind plagued by dark dreams of impending doom. In his fitful slumber, he found himself standing on the precipice of a great abyss, the cold winds of Tartarus whipping at his back as he gazed out into the darkness.

Before him, a shadowy figure emerged from the depths, its form twisted and distorted by the shifting shadows. It was Kronos, the ancient enemy of Olympus, and he spoke with a voice that echoed like thunder in the empty void.

"Tonight, we strike," Kronos growled, his eyes burning with a malevolent fire. "Under cover of darkness, we shall descend upon Camp Half-Blood like a shadowy tide, overwhelming their defenses and crushing their hopes of victory."

Andrew's heart pounded in his chest as he listened to Kronos' words, the weight of their meaning pressing down upon him like a suffocating blanket. He knew that the fate of Olympus hung in the balance, and that he and his companions were the last line of defense against the encroaching darkness.

With a start, Andrew awoke from his troubled sleep, his body drenched in a cold sweat as he struggled to shake off the lingering echoes of his dream. Beside him, his friends stirred restlessly, their faces drawn and tense as they prepared themselves for the battle to come.

With a sense of grim determination, Andrew and his companions set about preparing for the impending attack. Weapons were sharpened, armor donned, and battle plans hastily drawn up as they braced themselves for the coming storm.

As the minutes stretched into hours, the tension in the air grew palpable, each passing moment fraught with anticipation and dread. They knew that Kronos' forces would not hesitate to strike when the time was right, and that they must be ready to meet them head-on with all the strength and courage they could muster.

And so, as the first light of dawn began to creep over the horizon, casting long shadows across the camp, Andrew and his companions stood ready, their hearts filled with a steely resolve and a determination to defend their home and loved ones at any cost. For they knew that the battle ahead would be like none they had ever faced before, and that only by standing together could they hope to emerge victorious against the darkness that threatened to engulf them all.

As darkness descended upon Camp Half-Blood, the stillness of the night was shattered by the sound of approaching footsteps and the ominous rumble of an advancing army. Andrew and his companions sprang into action, their senses sharpened by the imminent threat as they prepared to face the darkness head-on.

With a resounding battle cry, Andrew led the charge, his sword held aloft as he surged forward to meet the enemy. His friends followed close behind, their weapons gleaming in the dim light as they fought with a fierce determination born of desperation and defiance.

The Titans' forces descended upon them like a tidal wave, their dark forms looming large in the moonlit night as they sought to overwhelm Camp Half-Blood's defenses. But Andrew and his companions stood firm, their resolve unshaken as they met the enemy with a ferocity that belied their years.

With each swing of their swords and each blast of their powers, they struck down their foes with precision and skill, their movements fluid and coordinated as they fought as one against the encroaching darkness. The ground trembled beneath their feet as the Titans' ranks were shattered by the sheer force of their onslaught, their cries of pain and rage drowned out by the cacophony of battle.

But even as they fought valiantly, Andrew knew that they could not hold out forever against the relentless tide of Kronos' forces. For every enemy they struck down, two more seemed to take its place, their numbers seemingly endless as they pressed ever closer to victory.

And yet, despite the odds stacked against them, Andrew and his companions refused to yield. With each passing moment, their determination only grew stronger, fueled by the knowledge that they fought not just for themselves, but for the future of Olympus itself.

But even as they battled on, the absence of the gods weighed heavily upon them. Without their divine guidance and intervention, they were left to fend for themselves against an enemy that seemed all but unstoppable.

But even as the darkness threatened to engulf them, Andrew and his companions stood their ground, their spirits unbroken as they fought with a courage born of desperation and defiance. For they knew that as long as they stood together, there was still hope for victory against the encroaching darkness that threatened to consume them all.

The clash of steel rang out through the night as Andrew and his companions fought on, their movements swift and precise as they engaged the enemy with all their might. With each strike of their weapons, they pushed back against the tide of darkness, determined to hold the line against Kronos' relentless onslaught.

Kiara, her powers over water unleashed in a torrential wave, swept aside the Titans with a ferocity that matched the crashing waves of the ocean. Adrian, his mastery of machinery at his command, unleashed a barrage of mechanical traps and devices that ensnared their enemies and turned the tide of battle in their favor.

Harry, his control over shadows growing stronger with each passing moment, wove a cloak of darkness around their enemies, obscuring their vision and sowing chaos among their ranks. And

Michael, ever steadfast at Andrew's side, fought with a courage and determination that inspired all who fought alongside him.

Together, they formed a formidable force, each member of the group contributing their own unique talents and abilities to the fight. With every foe they vanquished, they grew stronger, their resolve unshaken by the chaos and destruction that raged around them.

But even as they fought on, Andrew could sense that the battle was far from over. For every enemy they defeated, two more seemed to take its place, their numbers seemingly endless as they poured forth from the shadows to renew the assault.

Yet still, Andrew and his companions refused to yield, their spirits undaunted by the overwhelming odds stacked against them. With each passing moment, they fought with a renewed sense of purpose, their determination unyielding as they pressed forward into the heart of the enemy's ranks.

And as the first light of dawn began to break over the horizon, casting long shadows across the battlefield, Andrew and his companions stood victorious, their enemies vanquished and their home saved from destruction—for now, at least. But even as they celebrated their hard-won victory, they knew that the war was far from over, and that greater challenges lay ahead in their quest to defeat Kronos and save Olympus once and for all.

As the dust settled and the echoes of battle faded into the night, the weary demigods of Camp Half-Blood turned their thoughts to rest and recuperation. With the first light of dawn breaking over the horizon, they made their way back to camp, their steps heavy with exhaustion but their hearts light with the knowledge that they had emerged victorious against the forces of darkness.

The Apollo cabin, renowned for their healing abilities, sprang into action, their members working tirelessly to tend to the wounded and injured. With gentle hands and soothing words, they applied their knowledge of medicine and magic to ease the pain and suffering of their comrades, their golden light casting a warm glow over the wounded as they worked.

Under the watchful gaze of their counselor, the demigods of Apollo's cabin worked in harmony, their efforts guided by a sense of duty and compassion for their fellow campers. With each passing moment, the camp began to stir with new life, the sounds of laughter and conversation filling the air as the injured began to mend and heal.

But even as they worked to tend to the physical wounds of their comrades, the demigods of Apollo's cabin knew that the scars of war ran deeper than the surface. Many of their fellow campers bore the invisible wounds of battle—the trauma and loss that lingered long after the fighting had ended.

With gentle words of comfort and understanding, they offered solace to those who grieved, their presence a source of strength and support in the aftermath of the war. Together, they stood as a beacon of hope amidst the darkness, their unwavering dedication to healing and compassion serving as a testament to the resilience of the human spirit.

And as the sun rose high in the sky, casting its golden rays over the camp, the demigods of Camp Half-Blood came together once more, united in their shared triumph and bound by the bonds of friendship and camaraderie that had seen them through the darkest of times. For though the scars of war may linger, they knew that as long as they stood together, they could overcome any challenge that lay ahead.

In the quiet moments after the chaos of battle had subsided, Harry sought out Andrew, his expression grave and determined as he pulled him aside to share a secret plan.

"Andrew," Harry began, his voice low and urgent, "there's something I need to tell you. Something that could help us defeat Kronos once and for all."

Intrigued, Andrew listened intently as Harry outlined his plan, his eyes widening in surprise and disbelief at the daring scheme he proposed.

"The Achilles' Curse," Harry explained, his words tinged with a sense of both awe and dread. "Legend has it that Achilles, the greatest warrior of ancient Greece, was invulnerable to harm—except for one spot on his heel, where his mother held him when she dipped him in the River Styx."

Andrew's brow furrowed in confusion as he tried to make sense of Harry's words. "But how does that help us defeat Kronos?" he asked, his mind racing with possibilities.

Harry's expression grew grim as he continued. "Because the Achilles' Curse can be used as a weapon against him," he explained. "If we can obtain it and use it against Kronos, we may be able to weaken him enough to defeat him once and for all."

Andrew nodded slowly, the weight of Harry's words settling heavily upon him. The thought of facing Kronos in battle was daunting enough, but the idea of using such a powerful—and potentially dangerous—weapon against him filled him with a sense of both apprehension and determination.

But Harry's eyes burned with a fierce determination as he spoke, his voice filled with conviction. "We can do this, Andrew," he said, his words ringing with a sense of unwavering confidence. "We can defeat

Kronos and save Olympus from his tyranny. But we must act quickly, before it's too late."

With a nod of agreement, Andrew and Harry clasped hands in a silent vow of solidarity, their minds already turning to the daunting task that lay ahead. For they knew that the road to victory would be long and treacherous, but with courage, determination, and the strength of their friendship to guide them, they were ready to face whatever challenges lay ahead in their quest to save Olympus from destruction.

Chapter 6

THE CURSE

Under the shroud of night, Andrew and Harry embarked on a clandestine mission, their footsteps muffled by the hush of the sleeping camp. With determination etched into their faces, they made their way to the banks of the River Styx, where the waters churned with an otherworldly energy.

As they reached the edge of the river, Andrew turned to Harry, his eyes reflecting the weight of their shared purpose. With a silent nod, they exchanged a solemn understanding, knowing that what they were about to do would change the course of their destinies forever.

While Harry stood watch on the riverbank, Andrew prepared himself for the ritual ahead. With a steady hand and a resolute heart, he stepped into the icy waters of the Styx, feeling the chill seep into his bones as the currents enveloped him.

As he immersed himself in the dark waters, Andrew closed his eyes and focused his mind on the task at hand. With each passing moment, he could feel the curse of Achilles taking hold, granting him invincibility and strength beyond measure.

But even as the power surged through him, Andrew remained vigilant, mindful of the risks that came with such a formidable gift. With Harry's unwavering support by his side, he anchored his soul to the mortal realm, determined not to lose himself in the overwhelming tide of divine energy.

And then, with a final, desperate effort, Andrew emerged from the river, his body pulsing with newfound power and purpose. As he stood on the banks of the Styx, bathed in the pale light of the moon, he knew that he had achieved something truly extraordinary—a bond forged in the fires of adversity, a testament to his unwavering determination to protect all that he held dear.

With the curse of Achilles coursing through his veins, Andrew returned to Harry's side, his heart filled with a renewed sense of purpose. Together, they vowed to stand against the forces of darkness and defend their home at any cost, knowing that the fate of Olympus itself hung in the balance.

As Andrew emerged from the river, the first light of dawn began to paint the sky with hues of gold and pink. Blinking against the brightness, he found himself momentarily disoriented, the transition from darkness to daylight jarring in its abruptness.

"What... what happened to the night?" Andrew stammered, his voice tinged with confusion as he glanced around at the rapidly brightening landscape.

Harry, who had been keeping watch on the riverbank, approached Andrew with a knowing smile. "Time is different here," he explained calmly, his gaze meeting Andrew's with an unwavering certainty. "In the realm of the gods, moments can stretch into eternity, and seconds can pass like the blink of an eye."

Andrew's brow furrowed in contemplation as he processed Harry's words, the realization slowly dawning on him that the rules of mortal existence did not apply in this sacred realm. It was a humbling revelation, a reminder of the vast and incomprehensible power that lay beyond the realm of human understanding.

As the sun continued its ascent, bathing the world in its warm embrace, Andrew felt a sense of awe wash over him—a profound appreciation for the mysteries of the universe and the boundless possibilities that lay ahead. With Harry at his side, he knew that they were ready to face whatever challenges awaited them, armed with the knowledge that time itself was but a fleeting illusion in the grand tapestry of existence.

As Andrew and Harry stealthily made their way back into camp, the morning sun casting long shadows across the familiar paths, they were met with the curious gaze of Kiara, who had been anxiously awaiting their return.

Her brow furrowed in concern, Kiara stepped forward, her eyes flickering between Andrew and Harry as she took in their disheveled appearance and the tension that hung heavy in the air.

"Where have you two been?" she asked, her voice tinged with a mixture of worry and suspicion. "It's not like you to disappear like that without telling anyone."

Andrew exchanged a quick glance with Harry, a silent communication passing between them as they weighed their options. They knew that revealing the truth about their mission could put their friends in danger, but they also couldn't risk Kiara's trust by lying to her outright.

"We... we had something important to take care of," Andrew replied carefully, his words measured as he tried to convey the gravity of their situation without divulging too much information. "Something that couldn't wait."

Kiara's expression softened slightly at Andrew's earnest tone, but the furrow in her brow deepened as she sensed there was more to the story than he was letting on. She opened her mouth to press for further explanation, but Harry intervened before she could voice her suspicions.

"It's nothing you need to worry about, Kiara," Harry interjected, his voice calm and reassuring as he stepped closer to Andrew's side. "Just trust us when we say that we had good reason to be out there."

Kiara hesitated for a moment, her gaze shifting between Andrew and Harry as she weighed their words. Ultimately, she nodded in reluctant acceptance, her trust in her friends outweighing her need for answers.

"Alright," she conceded with a sigh, her voice softening with genuine concern as she reached out to squeeze Andrew's shoulder. "Just promise me you'll be careful. We're all counting on you."

Andrew nodded solemnly, a sense of gratitude welling up within him for Kiara's unwavering support. With a shared glance, he and Harry exchanged a silent vow to protect their friends and their home, no matter the cost. And as they turned to make their way back to their cabins, their resolve strengthened by Kiara's words, they knew that they were ready to face whatever challenges awaited them in the days to come.

As the trio made their way to the breakfast pavilion, the bustle of camp life surrounded them, the air alive with the chatter of demigods and the clatter of utensils against plates. The aroma of freshly cooked food wafted through the air, mingling with the scent of pine and the faint hint of magic that permeated the atmosphere.

As they approached the pavilion, Andrew couldn't help but feel a sense of comfort wash over him at the sight of his fellow campers gathered together, united by a common purpose and a shared sense of camaraderie. It was moments like these, amidst the hustle and bustle of camp life that reminded him of what they were fighting for— the bonds of friendship and the safety of their home.

Taking a seat at one of the long wooden tables, Andrew and his friends joined the throng of demigods, their presence met with nods of recognition and friendly smiles from their fellow campers. As they settled in to enjoy their meal, Andrew's thoughts turned to the challenges that lay ahead—the looming threat of Kronos and the impending battle that would determine the fate of Olympus.

But amidst the weight of their responsibilities, there was also a glimmer of hope—a belief that together, they could overcome any obstacle and emerge victorious against the forces of darkness. With his friends by his side and the support of their fellow demigods, Andrew knew that they stood a fighting chance against the greatest evil the world had ever known.

And as he dug into his breakfast, savoring the taste of home-cooked food and the warmth of friendship that surrounded him, Andrew felt a surge of determination fill his heart. Whatever trials lay ahead, he was ready to face them head-on, armed with the knowledge that he was not alone in his fight. Together, they would stand against the darkness and emerge stronger than ever before.

As the morning sun rose higher in the sky, casting a golden glow over the camp, Andrew and his companions witnessed the arrival of the demigods from Athens and Sparta, their figures silhouetted against the horizon as they made their way towards Camp Half-Blood.

With bated breath and hearts filled with anticipation, the campers watched as the demigods from the ancient cities approached, their numbers swelling with each passing moment. A sense of unity permeated the air as the newcomers joined the ranks of their fellow warriors, their presence adding to the growing sense of determination that hung thick in the air.

Andrew couldn't help but feel a surge of gratitude well up within him at the sight of their allies, knowing that their support would be invaluable in the days to come. He counted their numbers as they arrived, each new face a testament to the strength of their cause and the resilience of their people.

As the demigods from Athens and Sparta settled into camp, their arrival marked a turning point in their battle against Kronos and his forces. Their presence bolstered the spirits of their fellow campers, infusing the air with a renewed sense of determination and resolve.

With their numbers strengthened and their resolve fortified, Andrew knew that they were one step closer to victory. And as he looked out over the gathering of demigods, their faces lit with determination and courage, he couldn't help but feel a sense of hope swell within him.

For in the face of adversity, they stood united, ready to face whatever challenges lay ahead with unwavering resolve and unbreakable bonds of friendship. And as they prepared to confront the darkness that threatened to engulf them, Andrew knew that they would emerge stronger and more resilient than ever before.

Chapter 7

THE TITANS' FURY

As the sun dipped below the horizon, casting long shadows across the landscape, a sense of foreboding settled over Camp Half-Blood. The air crackled with tension as the demigods prepared for the inevitable clash with Kronos and his army of Titans.

Andrew stood at the forefront of the camp, his gaze fixed on the horizon where dark clouds gathered, a harbinger of the chaos to come. Beside him, his companions stood tall and resolute, their faces set with determination as they awaited the onslaught.

With a deafening roar, Kronos unleashed his full power, the ground trembling beneath their feet as the Titans surged forward, their monstrous forms blotting out the sky. Andrew and his companions braced themselves for the coming onslaught, their weapons at the ready as they prepared to defend their home and loved ones against the fury of the Titans.

The battle that ensued was like nothing they had ever faced before, a relentless onslaught of brute force and dark magic that tested their resolve to its limits. Andrew fought with all his might, his sword flashing in the fading light as he faced off against powerful foes, each one more formidable than the last.

But despite their courage and determination, the tide of battle soon turned against them as the Titans pressed their advantage, overwhelming them with their sheer numbers and raw power. Andrew and his companions fought valiantly, but it soon became clear that they were fighting a losing battle.

As the chaos raged around them, Andrew felt a surge of despair well up within him, the weight of their impossible task bearing down upon him like a heavy burden. But even in the darkest moments, he refused to give up hope, drawing strength from the unwavering courage of his friends and the knowledge that they fought not just for themselves, but for the future of Olympus itself.

With a rallying cry, Andrew pressed on, leading his companions into the heart of the fray as they fought tooth and nail against the relentless tide of darkness. Each blow struck was a testament to their determination, each victory won a step closer to turning the tide of battle in their favor.

But as the night wore on and the battle raged on, Andrew knew that their greatest challenge still lay ahead. With Kronos himself looming on the horizon, his dark presence casting a shadow over the battlefield, they would need to summon every ounce of strength and courage they possessed if they were to stand any chance of emerging victorious against the Titans' fury.

Chapter 7

THE TITAN'S FURY

As the demigods gathered at the base of the Empire State Building, a sense of urgency hung heavy in the air. Andrew scanned the faces of his comrades, his mind racing with the gravity of their mission. With a determined look, he began to assign each cabin a specific location to defend, his voice cutting through the clamor of the crowd.

"Apollo cabin, you're on the Brooklyn Bridge," Andrew announced, his voice steady despite the weight of his words. "Demeter cabin, guard the Manhattan Bridge. Ares cabin, you're holding down the Brooklyn-Battery Tunnel. Athena cabin, secure the Williamsburg Bridge."

He continued, allocating the cabins one by one to key points throughout the city. "Hermes cabin, you'll watch over the Queens-Midtown Tunnel. Hephaestus cabin, you're responsible for the Holland Tunnel. Dionysus cabin, your post is the 59th Street Bridge. And Aphrodite cabin, you'll defend the Lincoln Tunnel."

With each assignment, the demigods nodded in understanding, their expressions grim but resolute. They knew the importance of their roles in this battle for Olympus, and they were prepared to give their all to defend their home.

Meanwhile, the streets of Manhattan buzzed with activity as the city's inhabitants were swiftly evacuated, the mist cloaking their movements in the guise of an approaching storm. The mortal world remained oblivious to the impending battle that loomed on the horizon, shielded from the truth by the veil of the mist.

With their preparations complete and their defenses fortified, Andrew and his companions stood ready to face the Titans' fury head-on. As the sun dipped below the skyline, casting long shadows across the city, they braced themselves for the inevitable clash that would decide the fate of Olympus. And though the odds were stacked against them, they knew that as long as they stood united, they would never falter in their defense of their home.

As the demigods dispersed to their assigned posts, Andrew, Kiara, Harry, and Adrian embarked on their mission to defend the East River and the Hudson. With their weapons at the ready and their resolve steeled for battle, they made their way through the deserted streets of Manhattan, the weight of their task bearing down upon them.

The night air crackled with tension as they approached the East River, the waters shimmering in the moonlight as if anticipating the coming conflict. Andrew scanned the horizon, his senses alert for any sign of the enemy's approach. Kiara stood by his side, her eyes narrowed in determination as she readied her trident for battle.

Harry and Adrian flanked them, their presence a reassuring presence amidst the looming darkness. Together, they formed a formidable team, each member bringing their unique skills to bear in defense of their home.

As they reached the banks of the East River, a sense of foreboding washed over them, the silence of the night broken only by the distant sounds of approaching footsteps. They knew that their enemies were closing in, their intentions clear as they sought to claim victory over Olympus.

With a silent nod of understanding, Andrew and his companions braced themselves for the coming onslaught, their minds focused and their hearts steady. They would not falter in the face of adversity, for they were the champions of Olympus, and they would defend their home to the last.

As the first wave of enemies emerged from the shadows, Andrew raised his sword high, a battle cry echoing across the waters of the East River. With a fierce determination burning in their eyes, he and his companions charged forward to meet their foes, ready to face whatever challenges awaited them in the tumultuous night ahead.

As the enemy ships loomed on the horizon, their dark silhouettes cutting through the moonlit waters of the East River, Kiara stepped forward, her trident gleaming in the pale light. With a determined look in her eyes, she raised her weapon high, channeling the power of the sea as she prepared to unleash her wrath upon their foes.

With a mighty thrust of her trident, Kiara summoned a massive wave from the depths below, its frothing waters rising up to meet the enemy vessels with a deafening roar. The ships bucked and groaned as they were engulfed by the churning sea, their wooden hulls splintering under the force of Kiara's assault.

Andrew, Harry, and Adrian watched in awe as Kiara's power unleashed havoc upon their enemies, her command of the sea proving to be a formidable weapon in their arsenal. With each ship that succumbed to the fury of the waves, the demigods knew that they were one step closer to victory.

As the last of the enemy vessels disappeared beneath the tumultuous waters of the East River, Kiara lowered her trident, her chest heaving with exertion but her resolve unwavering. With a nod of satisfaction, she turned to her companions, a fierce determination burning in her eyes.

"The threat has been neutralized," Kiara declared, her voice ringing out across the waters. "But we must remain vigilant. The Titans will not rest until Olympus falls, and we cannot afford to underestimate their power."

With their enemies vanquished and their mission accomplished, Andrew, Kiara, Harry, and Adrian stood together on the banks of the East River, their spirits lifted by their hard-won victory. But even as they celebrated their triumph, they knew that the battle was far from over. The Titans still lurked in the shadows, biding their time until they could unleash their full fury upon Olympus once more. And it would be up to them, the champions of Olympus, to stand firm against the darkness and protect all that they held dear.

As the threat was neutralized and the waters of the East River calmed, Kiara raised her hand, signaling to the skies above. With a soft whinny and the beat of powerful wings, a group of majestic Pegasi descended from the heavens, their gleaming coats catching the moonlight as they landed gracefully on the riverbank.

Andrew, Kiara, Harry, and Adrian approached the winged creatures, their faces alight with anticipation as they prepared to take to the skies. With a sense of reverence, they each reached out to pat the creatures' necks, offering silent thanks for their aid in the battle against the Titans.

As Kiara whispered words of encouragement to the Pegasi, they knelt down, allowing the demigods to mount their backs. With a swift leap, Andrew, Kiara, Harry, and Adrian settled into the saddle, their hands gripping the reins tightly as they prepared for flight.

With a powerful thrust of their wings, the Pegasi launched into the air, their powerful muscles propelling them effortlessly into the night sky. As they ascended higher and higher, the lights of Manhattan spread out below them like a twinkling sea of stars, the city bathed in the soft glow of the moon.

Andrew glanced down at the bustling streets below, his heart swelling with pride at the sight of his home. But there was no time for sentimentality, not when the fate of Olympus hung in the balance. With a determined set to his jaw, he urged his Pegasus onward, leading the way as they soared over the city, their keen eyes scanning the horizon for any sign of trouble.

As they flew, Kiara, Harry, and Adrian spread out to cover as much ground as possible, their sharp eyes and keen senses alert for any signs of danger. Together, they flew in silent vigilance, their minds focused on the task at hand as they searched for any lingering threats to their home.

As Kiara called forth the Pegasi with a melodic whistle, the majestic creatures descended from the heavens, their powerful wings beating against the air as they touched down near the Brooklyn Bridge. Andrew and his companions wasted no time in mounting the winged steeds, their hearts heavy with the knowledge of the impending battle that awaited them.

With a gentle nudge from Kiara, the Pegasi took to the skies, carrying the four demigods high above the city of Manhattan. From their elevated vantage point, they surveyed the chaos unfolding below—the streets overrun with monstrous foes, the skyline painted with the fiery glow of conflict.

Hovering near the Brooklyn Bridge, Andrew's keen eyes spotted the Apollo cabin, their numbers engaged in a fierce struggle against the encroaching hordes of enemies. Without hesitation, Andrew directed the Pegasi to land near the embattled demigods, their hooves touching down softly on the pavement.

The Apollo campers looked up in surprise as Andrew and his companions dismounted, their expressions a mix of relief and determination. With a nod of acknowledgment, Andrew joined the fray, his sword flashing in the dim light as he waded into the thick of battle.

Beside him, Kiara unleashed torrents of water, sweeping away their adversaries with the force of a raging tide, while Harry and Adrian unleashed a barrage of fiery blasts and expertly crafted traps, driving back the enemy forces with skill and precision.

As the battle raged on, Andrew felt the power of the Achilles' curse coursing through his veins, granting him strength and agility beyond mortal limits. But even as he fought, a sense of unease lingered in the back of his mind—a reminder of the vulnerability that lay beneath his newfound invincibility.

But there was no time to dwell on doubts, not when lives hung in the balance and the fate of Olympus itself was at stake. With a fierce battle cry, Andrew pressed forward, his companions at his side, ready to face whatever challenges lay ahead in their quest to defend their home and their loved ones from the forces of darkness.

As the tide of battle began to turn in favor of the demigods, the monstrous horde began to retreat, their ranks thinning as they fled from the relentless onslaught of Andrew. But just when it seemed that victory was within their grasp, a fearsome roar shattered the relative calm of the battlefield, signaling the arrival of a new and deadly adversary.

The ground trembled beneath the weight of its massive form as the Chimera emerged from the shadows, its lion's head snarling with ferocious intensity, its serpent's tail thrashing with lethal intent, and its goat's head bleating with malicious glee.

The demigods exchanged uneasy glances, their hearts sinking with the realization that they faced a foe unlike any they had encountered before. The Chimera was a creature of legend, a monstrous hybrid born from the darkest depths of mythology, and its appearance on the battlefield struck fear into the hearts of even the bravest warriors.

But Andrew stood undaunted, his eyes blazing with determination as he faced down the Chimera with unwavering resolve. With a swift motion, he unsheathed his sword, its blade gleaming with the promise of impending battle, and prepared to meet the creature head-on.

The demigods watched in awe as Andrew charged forward, his movements fluid and precise as he closed the distance between himself and the Chimera in a matter of seconds. With a deft swing of his blade, he struck out at the creature, his strike finding its mark with unerring accuracy.

To the astonishment of all who bore witness to the spectacle, Andrew's blow proved to be true, piercing through the Chimera's defenses with deadly precision and striking true at the heart of the beast. With a final roar of defiance, the Chimera staggered back, its monstrous form collapsing to the ground in a heap of twisted limbs and shattered dreams.

The demigods stood in stunned silence, their eyes wide with disbelief as they watched Andrew emerge victorious from the fray, his sword held aloft in triumph. In that moment, they knew without a doubt that their leader was truly a force to be reckoned with—a hero destined for greatness, and a beacon of hope in the darkest of times.

As the battlefield fell into chaos, time itself seemed to slow to a crawl, the air crackling with the anticipation of impending conflict.

With a deafening roar, Kronos, the Titan of Time, emerged from the shadows, his towering form casting a dark shadow over the beleaguered demigods below.

Andrew met Kronos's gaze with steely determination, his grip tightening around the hilt of his sword as he prepared to face the greatest challenge of his life. With a thunderous clash of steel on steel, the two adversaries collided, their weapons sparking with the ferocity of their duel.

The demigods watched in awe as Andrew and Kronos traded blow for blow, their movements a blur of speed and skill as they danced across the battlefield. Each strike was met with a counter, each parry met with a riposte, as the fate of Olympus hung in the balance.

But as the battle raged on, it became clear that Kronos was a foe unlike any other, his mastery of time granting him an almost supernatural advantage over his mortal adversaries. With each passing moment, he seemed to grow stronger, his blows striking with the force of a titan unleashed.

Realizing that they were outmatched, Kiara quickly issued orders for the demigods of the Apollo cabin to retreat to the safety of the Empire State Building, their mission now to protect the entrance to Olympus at all costs.

As the demigods began their tactical withdrawal, Andrew and Kronos continued their fierce duel atop the Brooklyn Bridge, the structure groaning and creaking beneath the weight of their conflict. Sensing an opportunity, Andrew seized his chance, driving his sword deep into the weakened structure of the bridge itself.

With a deafening crack, the bridge gave way beneath them, the ground collapsing in a cascade of debris as the monstrous horde plummeted into the churning waters below. As the dust settled and the echoes of battle faded into the distance, Andrew looked on grimly, knowing that their victory had come at a heavy cost.

But even as Kronos made his escape, slipping through the cracks of time to fight another day, Andrew remained undeterred, his resolve stronger than ever as he turned his gaze toward the looming silhouette of the Empire State Building. For the war was far from over, and the fate of Olympus still hung in the balance.

As the dust settled and the remnants of battle scattered across the Brooklyn Bridge, Kiara approached Andrew, her expression a mix of awe and concern as she surveyed the aftermath of their harrowing encounter.

"Andrew, that was incredible," Kiara exclaimed, her voice tinged with admiration as she regarded her friend with newfound respect. "How did you... I mean, where did you get that kind of power?"

Andrew offered Kiara a wry smile, a flicker of amusement dancing in his eyes as he recounted the events that had led to his newfound abilities. "It's a long story," he began, his voice tinged with a hint of weariness as he recalled the trials and tribulations of their quest. "But let's just say that Harry and I stumbled upon something rather... unexpected."

With a sense of gravitas, Andrew proceeded to explain the nature of the Achilles' Curse, recounting how he had bathed in the River Styx and emerged with invulnerability and enhanced abilities, albeit with a single weakness that could prove fatal if exploited.

Kiara listened intently, her eyes widening in astonishment as she absorbed the gravity of Andrew's revelation. "So that's how you were able to hold your own against Kronos," she mused, a note of wonder in her voice. "But what about... you know, your Achilles' heel?"

Andrew nodded, his expression solemn as he raised his arm to reveal a small point on his elbow, barely visible beneath the fabric of his shirt. "This is it," he admitted, his voice tinged with a hint of vulnerability as he acknowledged the one weakness that could potentially undo him. "It's my only vulnerability, but I don't intend to let anyone exploit it."

Kiara regarded Andrew with a mixture of admiration and concern, her heart heavy with the weight of their shared burden. "We'll keep it safe," she promised, her voice resolute as she placed a hand on Andrew's shoulder. "No one will get past us, not while we're here to protect you."

With a nod of gratitude, Andrew returned Kiara's gaze, a sense of camaraderie passing between them as they reaffirmed their commitment to one another and to the cause they had sworn to defend. And as they turned their attention back to the task at hand, their resolve strengthened by their bond, they knew that together, they would face whatever challenges awaited them in the battles yet to come

Chapter 8

THE AFTERMATH

As the echoes of battle faded and the dust settled over the scarred landscape of Manhattan, Andrew found himself grappling with a myriad of emotions, his mind swirling with doubts and fears that threatened to consume him.

Alone amidst the ruins of the Brooklyn Bridge, he couldn't shake the nagging sense of uncertainty that gnawed at his insides. Despite their victory over Kronos and his forces, a shadow of doubt lingered in Andrew's heart, casting a pall over his triumph.

With a heavy sigh, Andrew sank to his knees, his thoughts a tumultuous whirlwind of confusion and despair. How could he, a mere demigod, hope to stand against the might of the Titans and their dark lord? Was he truly worthy of the mantle that had been thrust upon him, or was he destined to falter and fail in the face of such overwhelming odds?

But even as his doubts threatened to overwhelm him, a voice echoed in the depths of Andrew's soul, a voice filled with courage and determination—a voice that reminded him of all that he had fought for and all that he stood to lose.

Rising to his feet, Andrew squared his shoulders, his resolve hardening like steel as he cast aside his doubts and fears. He may not have all the answers, and he may not know what the future held, but he refused to let fear dictate his actions or dictate the fate of those he held dear.

With newfound determination coursing through his veins, Andrew set his sights on the task ahead, his mind clear and focused as he prepared to face whatever challenges awaited him. For the fate of Olympus hung in the balance, and he knew that he alone possessed the power to shape its destiny.

As he turned his gaze to the horizon, the first rays of dawn casting a golden glow over the ravaged cityscape, Andrew felt a surge of hope stir within him—a glimmer of light amidst the darkness that threatened to engulf them all.

And with that spark of hope burning bright within his heart, Andrew set out to confront his greatest fears and doubts, knowing that only by facing them head-on could he emerge stronger and more resolute than ever before.

For the battle may have been won, but the war was far from over. And as Andrew took his first steps into the uncertain future that lay ahead, he did so with the unwavering conviction that no matter what trials awaited him, he would face them with courage, honor, and the indomitable spirit of a true hero.

As the demigods gathered at the Empire State Building, their hearts heavy with the weight of loss and sacrifice, Andrew took charge, his mind already turning towards the daunting task that lay ahead. With solemn determination, he led his companions through the grim task of counting the casualties, each name a painful reminder of the cost of their struggle.

As the last of the fallen were tallied and the final toll of the battle was revealed, a somber silence fell over the assembled demigods, their faces drawn with grief and exhaustion. But even amidst their sorrow, there was a steely resolve in their eyes—a determination to honor the fallen by pressing forward in their fight against the Titans.

With a heavy heart, Andrew turned to his companions, his voice grave as he addressed them. "We've suffered great losses, but we cannot afford to dwell on our grief. The battle may be over, but the war rages on, and we must be prepared for what lies ahead."

Kiara nodded solemnly, her expression mirroring Andrew's grim resolve. "Agreed," she said, her voice firm with determination. "We cannot allow Kronos to continue unchecked. We must find a way to defeat him once and for all."

Harry and Adrian exchanged glances, their faces set in determined lines as they nodded their agreement. "We'll follow your lead, Andrew," Harry said, his voice steady despite the weariness etched into his features. "But we need to be smart about this. Kronos is too powerful for us to face alone."

Andrew nodded, his mind already racing with plans and strategies. "You're right," he said, his voice tinged with urgency. "We need help, and there's only one place we can turn to for that."

Turning towards the towering peak of Mount Olympus, Andrew's gaze hardened with determination. "We're going to Olympus," he declared, his voice ringing with conviction. "We'll consult the gods and seek their aid in our fight against Kronos. Together, we'll find a way to defeat him and save Olympus from his tyranny."

With a sense of purpose driving them forward, Andrew and his companions set out for the summit of Mount Olympus, their hearts heavy with the burden of their quest but filled with a fierce determination to succeed. For they knew that the fate of Olympus—and perhaps all of existence—hung in the balance, and they would not rest until they had done everything in their power to ensure its survival.

As Andrew and his companions ascended the towering slopes of Mount Olympus, the weight of their mission hung heavy upon their shoulders. With each step, they drew closer to the hallowed halls of the gods, where the fate of Olympus—and perhaps all of existence—would be decided.

As they reached the summit, they were met by the towering figures of the Olympian gods, their expressions grave as they listened to Andrew's account of the battle with Kronos and the dire threat he posed to their realm. Zeus, his countenance stern and unyielding, surveyed the gathered demigods with a keen gaze, his voice thundering like the crash of lightning as he addressed them.

"This is a grave matter indeed," Zeus rumbled, his voice echoing through the grand chamber of Olympus. "Kronos must be stopped at all costs. But the Titans are formidable foes, and we cannot face them alone."

Zeus, the king of the gods, regarded Athena with a measured gaze, his brow furrowed in contemplation. "And how do you propose we do that, daughter?" he inquired, his voice rumbling like distant thunder.

Athena's gaze shifted to Andrew and his companions, her eyes alight with determination. "We must elevate these brave demigods to the status of minor gods," she declared, her voice resonating with authority. "With the power and authority granted to them, they will be able to rally forces from across the mortal and immortal realms to our cause."

The other gods murmured amongst themselves, weighing the potential risks and rewards of Athena's proposal. Apollo, the god of prophecy, spoke next, his voice ringing out with clarity and foresight.

"It is a bold plan, sister, but one that may be our only hope," Apollo conceded, his expression grave. "The forces of Kronos grow stronger by the day, and we must match them in kind if we are to emerge victorious."

As Zeus summoned the three Fates, the atmosphere in the grand hall of Olympus grew tense with anticipation. The Fates, ancient and inscrutable, appeared before the assembly, their robes shimmering with threads of fate that wove through the fabric of existence.

Clotho, the spinner, with her spindle in hand, gazed upon Andrew and his companions with a knowing glint in her eyes. "The threads of destiny intertwine once more," she intoned, her voice carrying the weight of millennia. "The path of these mortals is veiled in shadow, yet their potential shines bright."

Lachesis, the measurer, stepped forward, her golden scales held aloft as she measured the strands of fate. "Their destinies are entwined with the tapestry of Olympus," she declared, her voice echoing through the hall. "Each thread woven with purpose, each choice leading them closer to their ultimate fate."

Finally, Atropos, the cutter, drew forth her shears, their blades glinting in the divine light of Olympus. "The time has come to reveal their true nature," she proclaimed, her voice resonating with finality. "Andrew Lancaster, son of Athena, you shall be known as the god of darkness, wielding the shadows as your weapon and shield."

Andrew's eyes widened in astonishment as the weight of his newfound divinity settled upon him. The mantle of godhood draped around his shoulders, imbuing him with power beyond mortal comprehension.

"Kiara Dean, daughter of Poseidon," Atropos continued, turning her gaze to Kiara with a solemn reverence. "You shall be the goddess of mazes, guiding mortals through the labyrinth of fate with wisdom and cunning."

Kiara's expression softened with a mixture of awe and determination as the realization of her divine calling washed over her. She stood taller, her presence imbued with the grace and strength of the sea itself.

"Harry Fletcher, son of Hades," Atropos intoned, her voice carrying a solemn weight as she addressed the young demigod. "You shall be the god of death, guiding souls to their final rest and wielding the power of the underworld with honor and compassion."

Harry's eyes shone with a fierce determination as he accepted his divine mantle, his resolve strengthened by the knowledge that he had been chosen for a purpose greater than himself.

"And Adrian McCall, son of Hephaestus," Atropos concluded, turning her gaze to the final member of the quartet. "You shall be the god of tools, shaping the world with your craftsmanship and innovation, forging the weapons and artifacts that will aid in the battle against darkness."

Adrian's hands tingled with divine energy as he accepted his newfound role, his mind already racing with ideas for inventions that would turn the tide of battle in Olympus' favor.

And as the Fates withdrew, their pronouncements echoing through the halls of Olympus, Andrew and his companions stood united, their destinies intertwined with the very fabric of the universe. With their newfound powers and the weight of Olympus behind them, they were ready to face whatever challenges lay ahead in their quest to save the world from the encroaching darkness.

Andrew, Kiara, Harry, and Adrian descended from the lofty heights of Olympus, their hearts brimming with newfound power and purpose. As they returned to the mortal realm, the weight of their divine mantles settled upon them like a mantle of strength and determination.

Gathering the demigods of Camp Half-Blood, Andrew stepped forward, his voice resonating with the authority of a god. "My fellow demigods," he began, his words carrying the weight of his newfound divinity. "We stand on the cusp of a great war, a battle that will determine the fate of Olympus and the world beyond."

Kiara, her eyes ablaze with the fire of her new role as goddess of mazes, stepped forward to join him. "But fear not, for we do not stand alone," she declared, her voice ringing with conviction. "With the blessings of the gods upon us, we are stronger than ever before."

Harry, his demeanor grave yet resolute, spoke next, his words carrying the weight of his newfound responsibility as god of death. "We have been chosen for a purpose," he proclaimed, his voice echoing with solemn determination. "To defend Olympus, to protect the mortal world, and to ensure that the light of hope never fades."

Adrian, his mind already racing with plans and inventions to aid their cause, added his voice to theirs. "And with our combined strength and ingenuity," he declared, his eyes shining with the spark of divine inspiration, "we shall forge the weapons and artifacts that will turn the tide of battle in our favor."

Together, the four newly anointed gods stood before their fellow demigods, their presence a beacon of hope in the gathering darkness. And as they shared their vision for the future, a sense of unity and purpose swept through the assembled campers, binding them together in a common cause.

For they knew that as long as they stood united, as long as they remained steadfast in their resolve, they would emerge victorious against whatever darkness threatened to engulf them. And with the blessings of the gods upon them, they were ready to face whatever challenges lay ahead in their quest to save the world from the encroaching shadows.

With a snap of his fingers, Adrian summoned forth a dazzling array of weapons, each one imbued with the power and craftsmanship of a god. Swords gleamed like shards of starlight, shields shimmered with an ethereal glow, and spears crackled with the energy of a thunderstorm.

As the demigods gazed upon the arsenal before them, a sense of awe and reverence filled the air. They reached out to claim their weapons, their hands trembling with anticipation as they felt the weight of divine power coursing through them.

Andrew, his eyes alight with determination, stepped forward to address his comrades. "These weapons are not just tools of war," he declared, his voice ringing with authority. "They are symbols of our strength, our unity, and our commitment to the cause."

Kiara nodded in agreement, her gaze sweeping over the assembled demigods. "With these weapons in our hands, we shall stand as guardians of Olympus and champions of justice," she proclaimed, her voice steady and resolute.

Harry, his expression grave yet determined, added his voice to theirs. "Let us wield these weapons with honor and courage," he urged, his eyes shining with the promise of battle. "For we fight not just for ourselves, but for the future of all."

And as the demigods prepared to take up their weapons and march into battle, a sense of purpose and determination settled over them like a cloak of invincibility. With their newfound strength and the blessings of the gods upon them, they were ready to face whatever challenges lay ahead in their quest to defend Olympus and preserve the world they called home.

With a firm resolve, Andrew rallied the demigods, his voice ringing out with clarity and authority as he outlined their plan of attack.

"We cannot afford to wait for Kronos to strike again," he declared, his eyes ablaze with determination. "We must take the fight to him, before he has a chance to regroup and strengthen his forces."

The demigods nodded in agreement, their faces set in grim determination as they prepared to march into battle once more. With their newly forged weapons in hand and the blessings of the gods upon them, they felt invincible, ready to face whatever challenges awaited them on the battlefield.

As they made their way towards the New York City Museum, the demigods moved with purpose and precision, their steps quickening with each passing moment. They knew that the fate of Olympus hung in the balance, and they were determined to emerge victorious, no matter the cost.

With Andrew leading the charge, the demigods advanced upon the enemy forces, their hearts filled with courage and determination. They knew that the battle ahead would be fierce and unforgiving, but they were ready to face whatever challenges awaited them, united in their quest to defend Olympus and preserve the world they held dear.

Chapter 9

THE FINAL STAND

As the demigods approached the New York City Museum, Andrew surveyed the scene before them with a mix of determination and apprehension. The museum loomed ahead, its grand façade a stark contrast to the chaos that awaited them within.

With a nod to his companions, Andrew signaled for them to form ranks, their weapons at the ready as they prepared to face Kronos and his minions head-on. The demigods fell into position, their faces set in grim determination as they braced themselves for the battle that lay ahead.

As they entered the courtyard of the museum, the air crackled with tension, the weight of their impending confrontation with Kronos hanging heavy upon them. Andrew's heart pounded in his chest as he stepped forward, his gaze locked on the titan who stood before them, a towering figure of darkness and destruction.

"Kronos," Andrew called out, his voice ringing out with authority as he addressed the titan. "I offer you one final chance to surrender. Lay down your arms and end this madness now, before more lives are lost."

But Kronos merely sneered in response, his eyes burning with hatred as he regarded Andrew and his companions with disdain. "Surrender?" he scoffed, his voice dripping with contempt. "I would sooner see Olympus reduced to rubble than bow to the likes of you, demigod."

With a heavy heart, Andrew knew that there would be no reasoning with Kronos. The titan was consumed by his lust for power and his desire to see Olympus fall, and no amount of pleading or negotiation would sway him from his path of destruction.

And so, with a solemn nod to his companions, Andrew prepared to lead them into battle. They had come too far to turn back now, and they would fight to the bitter end to defend their home and their loved ones from the forces of darkness.

With a rallying cry that echoed through the courtyard, Andrew lifted his sword high, the glint of determination shining in his eyes as he shouted, "FOR OLYMPUS!"

His voice was met with a chorus of echoing shouts from his companions, their battle cries mingling with the clash of weapons as they charged forward to meet their foes head-on. The ground trembled beneath their feet, the air crackling with energy as the forces of light and darkness collided in a storm of chaos and fury.

Andrew's heart pounded in his chest as he surged forward, his sword flashing in the sunlight as he engaged the enemy with unmatched ferocity. His every movement was a dance of skill and precision, his strikes finding their mark with deadly accuracy as he fought to defend all that he held dear.

Beside him, Kiara unleashed torrents of water upon their enemies, her powers of the sea surging forth with unparalleled force as she swept aside any who dared to stand in their way. Harry moved with a grace that belied his newfound power, his shadows weaving a deadly tapestry of death and destruction as he struck down foe after foe.

And Adrian, with his mastery of tools and machinery, unleashed a barrage of weapons upon their enemies, his creations tearing through the ranks of Kronos' minions with unstoppable force.

Together, they fought as one, their bonds of friendship and loyalty driving them forward even in the face of overwhelming odds.

With each swing of his blade, Andrew unleashed a wave of devastation upon the ranks of Kronos' minions. The curse of Achilles surged through him, infusing every movement with unparalleled power as he cut through his enemies with effortless precision.

The monsters stood little chance against his onslaught, their forms crumbling to dust with each strike of his sword. For every beast that dared to challenge him, two more fell to the ground in a shower of ash, their once formidable bodies reduced to nothing more than remnants of darkness.

Andrew's eyes blazed with determination as he pressed forward, his every movement a testament to the strength and resolve that burned within him. With each step, he carved a path of destruction through the enemy ranks, his comrades fighting at his side with equal fervor and determination.

The battlefield erupted into chaos as Andrew's relentless assault continued, the ground littered with the remains of fallen monsters as he surged ever onward. His companions followed in his wake, their weapons flashing in the sunlight as they fought to keep pace with his unstoppable onslaught.

As the battle raged on, Andrew's resolve only grew stronger, his determination to protect his home and loved ones driving him forward with unwavering purpose. With each enemy he vanquished, he drew closer to victory, his every action a testament to the power of courage and heroism in the face of darkness.

As Andrew slashed through the ranks of Kronos' army, he couldn't help but feel a sense of frustration mounting within him. For every monster he struck down with his sword, it seemed that two more emerged from the shadows to take its place, their relentless onslaught threatening to overwhelm even the most stalwart defenders of Olympus.

With each passing moment, the battlefield became a swirling maelstrom of chaos and confusion, the air thick with the stench of blood and the echoing cries of battle. Andrew fought with all his might, his every movement fueled by a burning determination to protect his home and those he held dear, but even his formidable skills were tested to their limits against the relentless tide of Kronos' minions.

As he surveyed the seemingly endless horde of monsters bearing down upon him, Andrew knew that they could not hope to defeat such overwhelming numbers through sheer force alone. They needed a strategy, a plan to turn the tide of battle in their favor before it was too late.

With a quick glance at his companions, Andrew nodded in silent agreement, his eyes alight with a fierce determination to prevail against the odds. Together, they would stand as one against the darkness, drawing upon their courage and resilience to face whatever challenges lay ahead.

With a steely determination burning in his eyes, Andrew stepped forward to face Kronos, his every movement radiating with an unwavering resolve as he prepared to confront the greatest threat to Olympus.

"Kronos," Andrew called out, his voice ringing clear and strong across the battlefield, "I challenge you to a duel, a test of strength and courage to determine the fate of Olympus."

Kronos regarded Andrew with a cold, calculating gaze, his lips twisting into a cruel smile as he accepted the challenge. "Very well, demigod," he replied, his voice dripping with malice, "but know this:

if you lose, your precious Olympus will fall, and there will be nothing to stand in my way."

Andrew squared his shoulders, his grip tightening around the hilt of his sword as he met Kronos' gaze with unwavering determination. "I understand the stakes," he declared, his voice steady despite the rising tension in the air, "and I swear upon the River Styx that I will abide by the outcome of our duel."

Kronos nodded in agreement, his eyes gleaming with a sinister light as he too swore the solemn oath. "Then let the duel begin," he proclaimed, his voice echoing across the battlefield as the two adversaries stepped forward to meet their destiny.

As Kronos summoned his scythe, a palpable tension settled over the battlefield. Andrew, undeterred, stood his ground, his grip tightening around the hilt of his sword as he prepared to face the Titan lord in combat. With a roar that echoed across the plains of battle, Kronos charged forward, his scythe cutting through the air with deadly precision.

Andrew met Kronos head-on, his movements fluid and precise as he deftly parried each strike with his own blade. The clash of their weapons reverberated through the air, the sound of steel on steel ringing out like a thunderous symphony.

With every swing of his scythe, Kronos unleashed waves of dark energy that crackled and sizzled with malevolent power. But Andrew, fueled by the determination to protect Olympus and all he held dear, fought with unmatched skill and courage.

Their duel raged on, each combatant pushing themselves to the brink of exhaustion as they exchanged blow after blow. As the minutes stretched into hours, the battlefield became a swirling maelstrom of chaos and destruction, with Andrew and Kronos at its epicenter.

As the clash of titans reverberated through the battlefield, Andrew, now empowered by his newfound divinity as the God of Darkness, summoned forth his most potent weapon—the legendary Sword of Darkness. Forged in the depths of the abyss and steeped in the ancient power of the primordial shadows, this weapon was a harbinger of destruction, capable of sundering even the mightiest of foes.

With a gesture of his hand, the air crackled with dark energy as the Sword of Darkness materialized before him, its obsidian blade gleaming with an ominous radiance. Andrew grasped the hilt firmly, feeling the pulsating energy of the weapon course through his veins, filling him with an almost primal sense of power.

Across the battlefield, Kronos, the ancient Titan lord, raised his scythe—a grim harbinger of death and despair—as he prepared to face his divine adversary. With a roar that echoed across the heavens, he charged forward, his form wreathed in swirling shadows as he unleashed a barrage of devastating blows.

But Andrew, fueled by the inexorable force of the shadows, met Kronos head-on, his movements swift and decisive as he parried each strike with uncanny precision. With each clash of their weapons, the very fabric of reality seemed to tremble, as if the fate of the cosmos hung in the balance.

As the battle reached its climax, Andrew channeled the full power of the Sword of Darkness, unleashing a torrent of dark energy that engulfed Kronos in a maelstrom of shadows. With a mighty thrust, he drove the blade deep into the heart of his adversary, piercing the Titan's essence with an irrevocable finality.

With a deafening roar, Kronos' form began to unravel, his shadowy essence dissipating into the void as the echoes of battle faded into silence. As the dust settled and the battlefield fell silent,

Andrew stood triumphant, the Sword of Darkness held aloft as a testament to his indomitable will and unyielding resolve.

And as the sun rose once more over the blood-stained fields of battle, Andrew knew that the war was won, but the true test of his newfound power had only just begun. As the God of Darkness, he would be called upon to face even greater challenges in the days to come.

Chapter 10

INTO THE ABYSS

In the grandeur of Mount Olympus, where the celestial hues of dawn painted the sky with strokes of molten gold and fiery crimson, Andrew and his steadfast companions embarked on a journey that transcended mortal reckoning. Their footsteps, though heavy with the weight of their recent victory, echoed resolutely against the polished marble floor of the Olympian hall as they approached the imposing throne of Zeus, the sovereign deity presiding over all.

Each member of the party bore the scars of their arduous odyssey, a testament to the trials endured and the sacrifices made in the name of Olympus. Their voices, hoarse but unwavering, recounted the epic clash against the tyrannical Kronos, detailing their valor and ultimate triumph over the forces of darkness that threatened to engulf the realm of gods and mortals alike.

As their narration unfolded, a profound solemnity settled upon the assembly of deities, their immortal countenances reflecting the gravity of the sacrifices made to safeguard their divine domain. Though victory had been achieved, its cost lingered like a shadow, a poignant reminder of the toll exacted by the relentless march of fate.

Yet, within the somber atmosphere, a flicker of warmth stirred – a nascent sense of unity and shared purpose that transcended the encroaching darkness. In the crucible of adversity, demigods and gods had stood as equals, their resolve serving as a beacon of hope amidst the chaos.

As Andrew and his companions concluded their narration, a wave of appreciation washed over them from the Olympian assembly. The austere visages of the gods softened marginally, replaced by a grudging respect for the valor displayed by mortals in the face of insurmountable odds. Athena, with eyes akin to piercing gray stones, offered a curt nod of acknowledgment, while Apollo, with his golden lyre catching the ethereal light, strummed a melody of triumph in their honor.

Even Zeus, the mighty king of gods, could not entirely conceal a flicker of approval in his typically stern countenance as he acknowledged their courage and unwavering determination. "You have proven yourselves worthy defenders of Olympus," his voice resounded like thunder, carrying the weight of divine authority. "Your valor and sacrifice shall echo through the annals of time."

A chorus of agreement rose from the other gods, their voices a symphony of validation that enveloped Andrew and his companions, infusing them with a renewed sense of purpose. Though the path ahead remained obscured by uncertainty, they took solace in the unwavering support of the divine pantheon, a guiding light illuminating the darkness of the unknown.

With a deep bow of gratitude, their voices resonating with sincerity, Andrew and his companions expressed their thanks to the assembled deities. As they turned to depart the grand hall, Apollo's voice resonated once more, his words carrying an otherworldly resonance that commanded the attention of all present.

"In the shadows' grasp, the claimer shall rise, Their grip unyielding, dominion in their eyes. Olympus shall falter, its glory laid to rest, As the new dawn yields to the Darkblade's test."

The prophecy reverberated through Andrew like a clarion call, sending a chill down his spine. He tightened his grip on the sword of darkness, its obsidian blade shimmering ominously in the dim light. This very weapon, seized during the conflict, now pulsed with a power that threatened to consume him.

A hushed silence descended upon the assembly as the weight of the prophecy settled upon them. Andrew felt the collective gaze of the gods upon him, their eyes a mixture of awe and trepidation. He understood – he was the prophesied claimer, the harbinger of change destined to shape the fate of Olympus and beyond.

Before Athena could voice her concern, Zeus raised a hand, quelling any dissent. The air crackled with tension as all eyes fixated on the king of gods, his expression an unyielding mask of determination.

"Silence, Athena," his voice thundered, commanding obedience from all. "This matter transcends your apprehensions."

Though Athena's lips tightened with defiance, she acquiesced, her gaze lingering on Andrew with a blend of sorrow and resolve.

Turning back to Andrew, Zeus's eyes blazed with a chilling resolve as he delivered his decree. "You and your companions have wielded a power that threatens the very fabric of Olympus. For the safety of all, I have no choice but to exile you... to the depths of Tartarus."

The weight of Zeus's judgment crashed upon Andrew, igniting a fiery rage within him. His voice, quivering with righteous indignation, rose to challenge the king of gods.

"Exile us?" he thundered, his eyes ablaze with defiance. "We fought to protect Olympus, to safeguard the very gods who now cast us aside like mere mortals! But heed my words, Zeus – this is not the end. If you cast us out, then we shall return, and Olympus shall tremble!"

His declaration reverberated through the grand hall, a stark challenge echoing through the hallowed chambers. Beside him, Kiara, Harry, and Adrian stood unwavering, their faces etched with grim determination, ready to face whatever fate awaited them.

Unfazed by Andrew's outburst, Zeus raised a hand, his expression hardening further. A low rumble emanated from beneath the marble floor, growing louder with each passing moment. A swirling vortex of inky darkness materialized at the heart of the hall, its edges crackling with an ominous energy.

"So be it," declared Zeus, his voice resolute. "For the preservation of Olympus, you are banished to the depths of Tartarus."

As Andrew surged forward, fury coursing through his veins, an unseen force propelled him backward. Kiara, Harry, and Adrian were similarly cast towards the vortex, their cries swallowed by the growing roar of the abyss.

With a final, desperate glance at the impassive visages of the gods, Andrew felt himself torn from the only home he had ever known. The world dissolved into a chaotic whirl of darkness, the anguished screams of his companions serving as the only tethers to his rapidly unraveling sanity.

They plummeted through the infinite abyss, a harrowing descent into the very bowels of the earth. The air grew thick and oppressive, tainted with the stench of decay and despair. Bioluminescent fungi cast an eerie glow upon the cavern walls, revealing grotesque shapes that writhed and pulsated in the shadows.

Finally, with a bone-jarring impact, they crashed upon a rugged, uneven surface. Groaning as he struggled to his feet, Andrew surveyed their surroundings. They stood within a vast cavern, a desolate landscape bathed in the feeble glow of phosphorescent flora. In the distance, the primal roars of unseen monstrosities reverberated through the subterranean expanse, sending shivers down Andrew's spine.

Kiara, her countenance pale yet resolute, staggered upright. "We yet draw breath," she rasped, clutching her side where an unseen blow had landed. Harry and Adrian, dusted with grime but otherwise unscathed, joined her, their expressions a blend of trepidation and defiance.

"Tartarus," Harry murmured, awe lacing his voice. "A realm reserved for the most perilous denizens of existence. And now, us."

Andrew tightened his grip on the hilt of the sword of darkness, a surge of primal power coursing through him. Uncertain of the trials that lay ahead, one thing remained immutable: they would not languish as captives in this forsaken realm. He met the gazes of his companions, their eyes reflecting a shared determination.

"Though banished we may be," he proclaimed, his voice ringing with resolve, "our spirits remain unbroken. Whatever perils this realm may hold, we shall endure. We shall find a means of escape. And when we emerge from the depths, Olympus itself shall quake beneath our defiance."

A flicker of hope ignited within them, a beacon of rebellion against the gods who had betrayed their trust. In the desolate depths of Tartarus, a new purpose took root – not merely survival, but vengeance. Their journey had veered into darkness, yet Andrew and his stalwart companions remained undeterred. Their quest for justice had only just begun.

Don't miss out!

Visit the website below and you can sign up to receive emails whenever Tharun Vigneswar PS publishes a new book. There's no charge and no obligation.

https://books2read.com/r/B-A-LBUIB-YHZDD

BOOKS2READ

Connecting independent readers to independent writers.

Also by Tharun Vigneswar PS

Andrew Lancaster and The Olympians
Darkness Rising
Legacy of Darkness